THIS BOOK IS DEDICATED TO MY ONE AND ONLY SON JUDAH. CONTINUE TO BE GREAT AND LISTEN TO GOD'S VOICE. ALWAYS KNOW THAT YOU ARE IMPORTANT AND LOVED.

LOVE FOREVER,
MOMMY

Copyright © 2020 by Tiana Williams
Illustrations by Whimsical Designs by CJ, LLC

Published by TT&J UNLIMITED

Printed in the United States of America
First Printing, 2020
ISBN 978-1-7350439-0-6

The ADVENTURES OF
JUDAH the GREAT:
Who am I?

Written by
Tiana Williams

&

Illustrated by
Whimsical Designs by CJ

How did you get so BIG and STRONG, brown like the earth with a voice so powerful..

He is strong and his Word is the truth. I have learned to speak to all things and watch my words come true.

His mind and thoughts are mine.

As long as I think on *Him*, learn of *Him* and believe in *Him* I will forever be sound.

We were created to be just like *Him*...

... yes, you and me too.

Don't be afraid
for fear will never
work.

Hold your head high even
when you feel down.

For the *Holy Spirit* will give you peace and *He* is always around.

Now, who am I you ask?
I am the voice that removes
doubt and the love that is dear.

I have a soul.
Not the kind of soul
that makes you dance...

Although, I feel like dancing at the mention of *His* name.

My soul is sometimes *happy*, *sad*, or *mad*.

It is my feelings.

Feelings are important and can allow you to be mad with friends during games.

Then it can all change and you will
be glad to hear your friend's names.

I am not my body.

NO I AM NOT!

My body has a function
and it may not be what you thought.

My body is a house for my
soul to live in.
It is my skin.
The skin I am in is not who I
am or all I will be.

It is just the shelter
and allows me to move
and carry out *His* word
on this earth.

Who am I you ask?

I am a *spirit*.

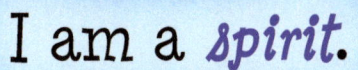

I am a *spirit* that
God placed in a body.

I can help others and do good deeds.

I have a soul that I can control.

No tempers or sadness
because *Love* is the key.

So who am I
you ask?

I am **EVERYTHING**

He needs me to be.

Scriptures (King James Version)

Galatians 2:20 "I am crucified with Christ: nevertheless I live; yet not I, but Christ liveth in me: and the life which I now live in the flesh I live by the faith of the Son of God, who love me, and gave himself for me."

Romans 8:9 "But ye are not in the flesh, but in the Spirit, if so be that the Spirit of God dwell in you. Now if any man have not the Spirit of Christ, he is none of his."

Philippians 2:5 "Let this mind be in you, which was also in Christ Jesus:"

Genesis 1:26 "And God said Let us make man in our image, after our likeness:"

Genesis 2:7 "And the Lord God formed man of the dust of the ground, and breathed into his nostrils the breath of life, and man became a living soul."

www.ingramcontent.com/pod-product-compliance
Lightning Source LLC
Chambersburg PA
CBHW040333260626
47164CB00020B/102